W9-CDJ-608

Rhino Romp

by Jean Craighead George

Illustrated by Stacey Schuett

New York

Simu was resting in the heat of midday. He was sparsely shaded by his splendid one-and-a-half-ton mother and his loving one-and-a-half-ton aunt.

Simu was not sleeping. He was looking over the curve of the biggest of his mother's two horns as he watched the savanna for someone to play with. He was almost a year old with an insatiable need to have fun.

As far as he could see, which was not very far, there was no one to play with, not even his chasing partner Zella, a young gazelle. As far as he could hear, which was very far, there were only deep breathings from sleeping and resting neighbors.

The temperature dropped a few degrees, and Simu got up. He shook the dust from his hide. His favorite toy, a big stick, lay nearby. He charged, picked it up with his big nose, and tossed it. He charged it again, then stopped still.

He heard big, big playtime coming his way. A squeaking of wing feathers told him Tilo, the marabou stork, had just made a landing. He loved Tilo. She was his very favorite chasing partner. Simu lifted his tail in joy, pressed down on his three-toed feet, and trotted to meet Tilo.

She ran. Simu ran after her. Chasing was what Simu was born for.

Tilo led Simu around a baobab tree, into thorn bushes, and across the savanna toward Simu's father. He was far out in the tall-grass savanna, defending their territory against other white rhinos.

Suddenly Tilo stopped and faced Simu. She lifted her huge wings and rattled her throat in annoyance. She was building a nest in the stork roost. She did not want to play anymore. Simu frolicked toward her. Tilo jumped, flew, and ran toward the trees. Tossing his head, Simu galloped after her.

Tilo led Simu past a herd of elephants. Simu stopped and looked at them. They were bigger than his enormous father. They are the only land animals in the world bigger than white rhinos, and Simu was impressed. He twirled his ears and sniffed the elephants. A protective mother rushed at him.

Simu was very fast. He galloped away and caught up with Tilo. She was among a herd of zebras, picking up a stick for her nest.

The zebras saw the thousand-pound Simu running toward them. They turned their hindquarters, ready to kick him to pieces. Simu fled.

A secretary bird burst up as he ran. He chased her. Helmeted guinea hens scattered before him. He chased them. This was fun. He dashed, turned, and ran. Simu was fat and square but very agile. He scared up a kori bustard and chased her.

When he stopped he did not know where he was. He could not smell his mother or aunt. He could not see Tilo or the baobab tree. He was lost.

Simu looked around. The elephants, zebras, and gazelles were running toward the horizon. The wildebeests were galloping after them. The vultures were flying off. The guinea fowl were crying their warning calls. Even a gang of fearless spotted hyenas dashed away.

Simu was frightened for the first time in his life. Something terribly dangerous was happening. All the animals but him knew what it was. He stood still. The earth shook under his feet.

Coming over the horizon was a cloud of dust. It sped toward him at twenty-five miles per hour. He trembled. The cloud of dust shrieked.

Suddenly Simu lifted his tail in excitement. Out of the cloud of dust roared his mother and aunt. A one-and-a-half-ton mother and a one-and-a-half-ton aunt protecting their baby are a menace. Not a wildebeest or vulture or hyena or even an elephant was anywhere to be seen.

Simu ran to his mother. They gently greeted each other nose-to-nose.

His mother led him with her fast high-stepping trot into the reeds. He sniffed them and swirled his tail in joy. He was on their path to the wallow. He ran full speed ahead.

With a belly flop Simu splashed into the brown wallow water and sank up to his chin in mud.

He squealed with pleasure. Wallowing was the most wonderful of all rhino games. He rolled in the mud and grunted. His mother and aunt wallowed beside him while his father went on defending their territory far out on the greening savanna.

Simu sighed with big contentment. He had had a big romp, he was having a big mud bath, and he had a big, watchful mother and aunt.

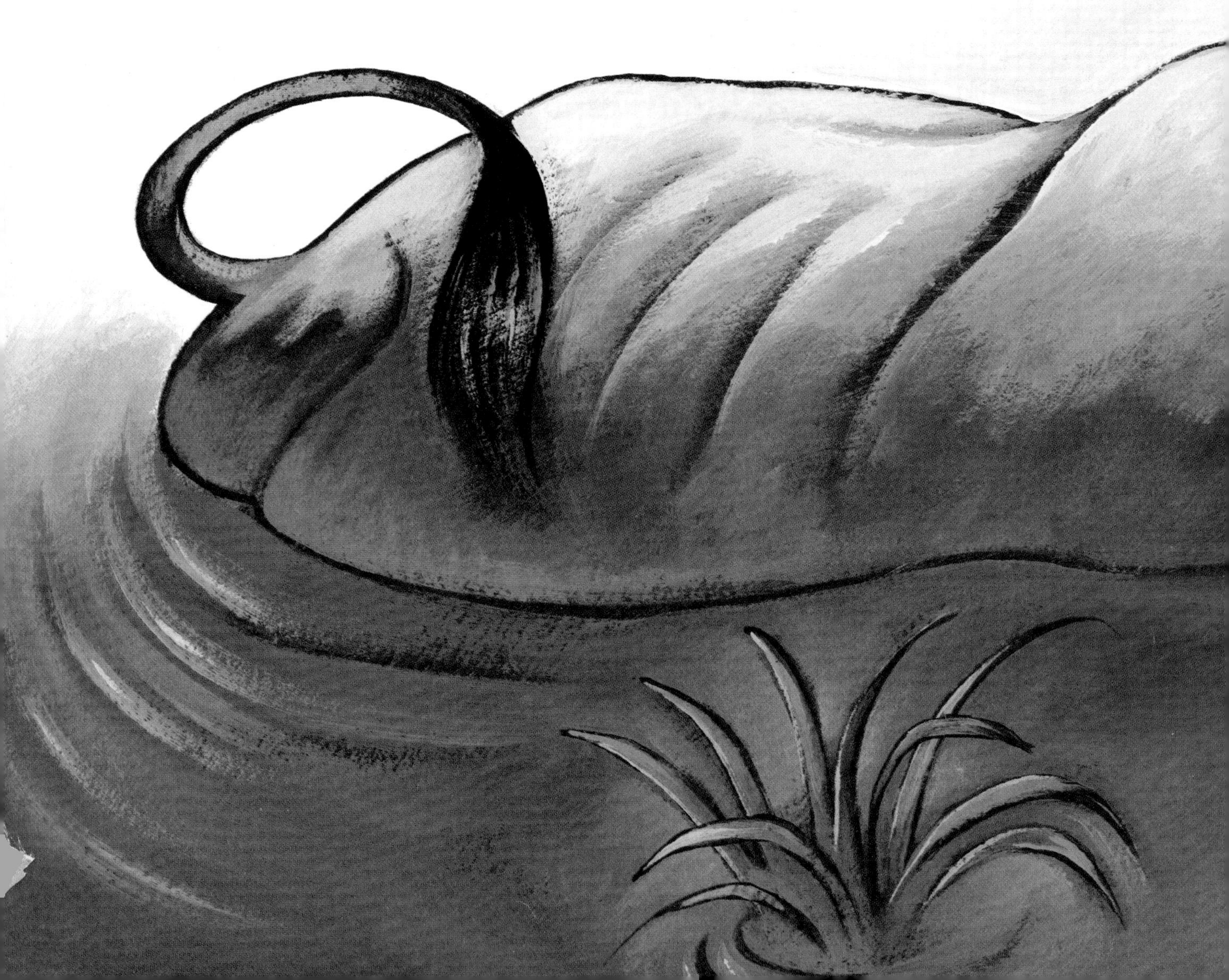

Cast of Characters

SIMU
WHITE RHINOCEROS
scientific name:
Ceratotherium simum

The Swahili word for "wide" is "whyte," hence the name white rhino. These rhinos have wide, wide mouths compared to the black rhino. There is no color difference.

TILO
MARAGOU STORK
Simu's chasing friend
scientific name:
Leptoptilos crumeniferus

The marabou stork is an enormous African bird. The head is naked and red, its neck naked and pink with a few wispy feathers. It has a cowlike bellow and wings that make loud squeaking noises during takeoff and landing. Twenty to many thousands nest in colonies in trees or on cliffs.

ZELLA
GRANT'S GAZELLE
Simu's chasing friend
scientific name: *Gazella granti*

Grant's gazelle is a large African gazelle with a white rump and a vertical dark stripe on each side. Its horns are large, graceful, and thick. It roams in small herds: about nine females and young with one male. Bachelor males form smaller herds.

ELEPHANT
Simu's forest-edge neighbor
scientific name: *Loxodonta africana*

The African elephant is the largest land mammal. A male weighs about five tons, a female almost four. Their ivory tusks are so valuable they have been hunted almost to extinction. One calf is born after a twenty-two-month gestation period, the longest of any mammal. The calves and their mothers stay in a group led by the biggest and oldest cow.

ZEBRA
Simu's savanna neighbor
scientific name: *Equus burchelli*

The zebra resembles a sturdy pony, decorated with handsome black or brown stripes that distinguish it from all other beasts. A male weighs about 550 pounds, the female about 480. They give birth to one foal after a twelve-month gestation.

SECRETARY BIRD
Simu's savanna neighbor
scientific name: *Sagittarius serpentarius*

The secretary bird is the "eagle of the African savannas." It sports long legs and feathers on the nape of its neck that look like quill pens, hence its name. Up to six of these birds will perform a courtship dance together with their wings held up. They build stick nests in short thorny trees.

KORI BUSTARD
Simu's open-grassland neighbor
scientific name: *Ardeotis kori*

The kori bustard is one of the world's largest flying birds, so large it doesn't fly much but wanders on the ground eating grasshoppers, reptiles, rodents, seeds, roots, and wild melons. The male has a deep lionlike voice.

HELMETED GUINEA FOWL
Simu's wooded-grassland neighbor
scientific name: *Numida meleagris*

A helmeted guinea fowl is black with white spots all over it. Blue, white, and red skin covers the head. A bony casque on the crown inspired the name "helmeted." The males fight viciously for mates, and the females lay as many as twelve eggs in a ground nest lined with feathers.

SPOTTED HYENA
Simu's savanna neighbor
scientific name: *Crocuta crocuta*

The spotted hyena is doglike but more closely related to the mongoose. They are predators and scavengers. They have big teeth and can run down and kill a bull wildebeest. One or two cubs are born after a four-month gestation.

Disney is committed to wildlife conservation worldwide. At Disney's Animal Kingdom, most of the animals that guests will see were born in zoological parks. A safari adventure ride features live animals in a re-creation of the African savanna. Guests can also visit Conservation Station, the headquarters for conservation and species survival activities.

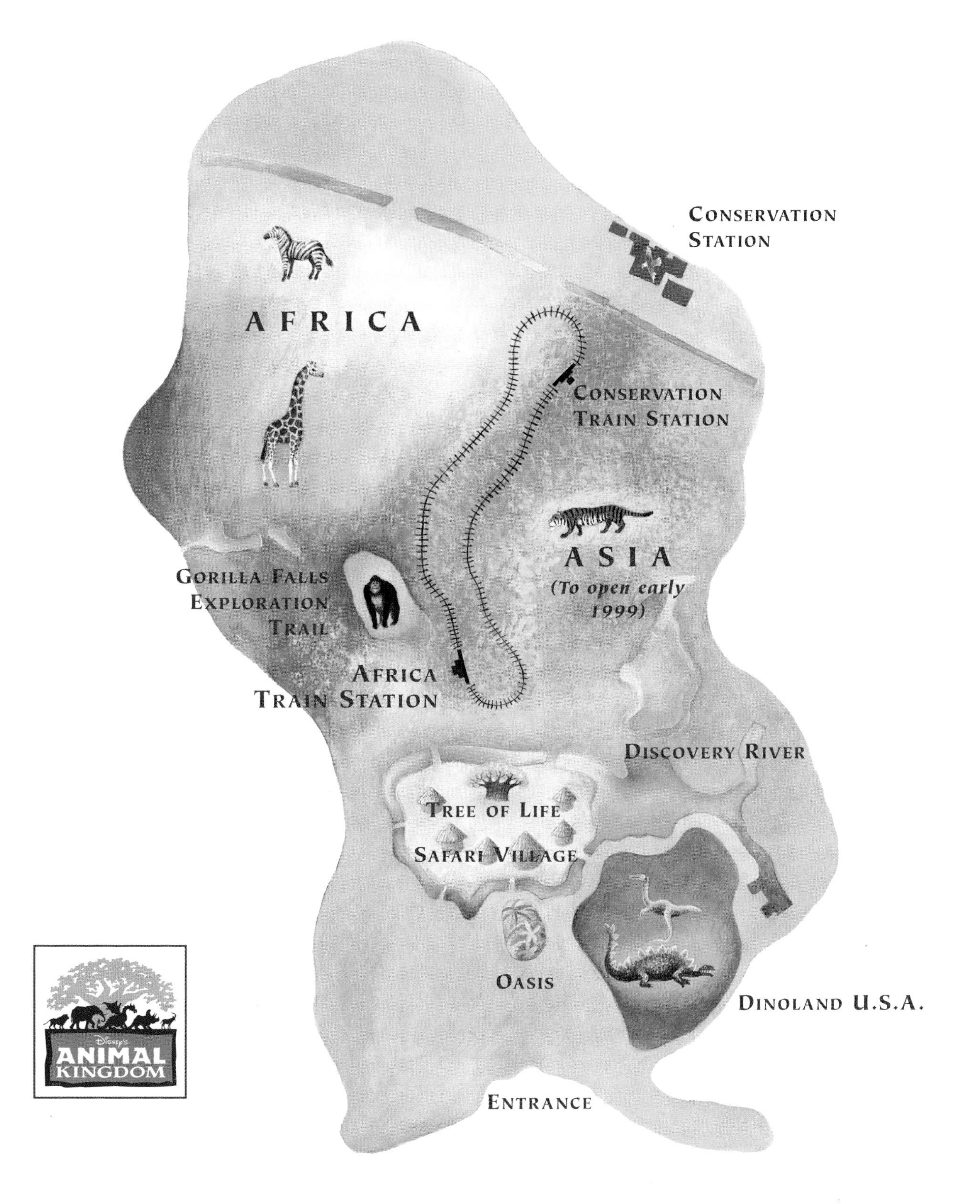
Conservation
Station
Africa
Conservation
Train Station
Asia
(To open early
1999)
Gorilla Falls
Exploration
Trail
Africa
Train Station
Discovery River
Tree of Life
Safari Village
Oasis
Dinoland U.S.A.
Entrance
Disney's
Animal
Kingdom

To Charlotte– J.C.G.

To Frances K., with thanks– S. S.

Printed in the United States of America.

The text for this book is set in 16-point Tiepolo.
The artwork for each picture was painted with watercolors.

Library of Congress Catalog Card Number: 97-80238
ISBN: 0-7868-3164-2 (trade)—ISBN: 0-7868-5068-X (lib. bdg.)